The SEVEN RAVENS

By the Brothers Grimm

Adapted by Laura Geringer • Paintings by Edward S. Gazsi

📚 HarperCollins*Publishers*

The great appeal of this story to me as a child resided in the strength and bravery of the little girl heroine who, though born sickly and small, takes on the task of going out alone into the world to find her lost brothers. Inspired by love, by faith in forgiveness, and by the powerful desire for a family that is whole, she faces the forces of nature and the harshness of the elements.

The basic plot of *The Seven Ravens* appears in all the major collections of fairy tales by the Brothers Grimm. Translations by Ralph Manheim, Margaret Hunt, and Jack Zipes have essentially the same events. In each, the father loses his temper and lets fly the curse that transforms his male children. In each, his daughter takes from home the comforting loaf of bread, jug of water, and little stool. In each she encounters the sun, the moon, and the stars. The round boy, the goat and shepherdess, the baby rattle, the embroidered shirts, and the glass bone are my own inventions (though the discovery of shirts in a similar revelation appears briefly in another Grimm tale, "The Twelve Brothers"). In the original story the girl must sacrifice one of her fingers to gain entry into the Glass Mountain, an event I eliminated, choosing to emphasize instead the psychological sacrifice of growing up in a household that harbored so dark and shadowy a secret.

—Laura Geringer

Library of Congress Cataloging-in-Publication Data
Geringer, Laura.
    The seven ravens / by the Brothers Grimm ; adapted by Laura Geringer ; paintings by Edward S. Gazsi.
        p.   cm.
    Summary: A little girl walks to the end of the world to find her seven brothers and free them from enchantment.
    ISBN 0-06-023552-7. — ISBN 0-06-023553-5 (lib. bdg.)
    [1. Fairy tales.   2. Folklore—Germany.]   I. Grimm, Jacob, 1785–1863.   II. Grimm, Wilhelm, 1786–1859.   III. Gazsi, Edward S., ill.   IV. Title.   V. Title:
7 ravens.
PZ8.G3324Se   1994   93-8161
398.21—dc20   CIP
                                                                                                                              AC

Typography by Christine Kettner
1   2   3   4   5   6   7   8   9   10
❖
First Edition

For my brother, with love

—L. G.

To my children, Jeremiah, Jessica, Jonathan, and Justin.
Each has endured in good humor the rigors of modeling
for countless projects, from the sublime to the ridiculous.
"Behold, children are a gift from the Lord. How blessed
is the man whose quiver is full of them."

—E. S. G.

HERE WAS ONCE a baby girl as beautiful as the sun is hot, as brave as the moon is cold, and as gentle and faithful as the stars are bright. Her parents loved her very much. Yet as she grew, she saw that they were not happy.

In the mornings, her mother would sing as she brushed her daughter's long dark hair, but her songs were sad. In the evenings, her father would laugh as he lifted her high above his head into the air. But when she looked into his eyes, she saw shadows there.

One day, while chasing a ball, the little girl crawled under her parents' bed and came upon seven dusty boxes. She opened them and found in each a neatly folded shirt, delicately sewn in colors of the rainbow with patterns of the sun, moon, and stars. They were so finely embroidered, only her mother could have made them.

That night at dinner, the girl wore the smallest of the shirts, hoping to make her mother smile. But when her mother saw it, she covered her face with her hands. And her father began to weep.

"Your poor brothers," they moaned, rocking back and forth. "Your poor, poor brothers."

And so her parents told the little girl of a time when they had seven strong sons, each more handsome than the last.

"Soon after you were born," said her mother, "you fell ill—so ill we feared you might die. We asked the boys to be very quiet when they came near your cradle, but they forgot our warnings. One day, while playing, they woke you from a sound sleep.

"'I wish you'd all turn into ravens and fly away!' cried your father in a rage.

"Lo and behold! Seven birds as black as night surrounded you in a great whir of wings. The largest dipped down, plucked the rattle from your hand, and holding it in his beak, rose up again, leading the others."

"They disappeared into the clear blue sky," said her father. And as he spoke, the girl counted seven black shadows in his eyes.

"I'll find them," she promised, resting her head on her father's shoulder. "I'll bring them home."

"What's done is done," he whispered, shaking his head slowly. And the shadows in his eyes seemed to spread through the house, filling every crack and corner.

That night, the little girl could not sleep. She had been spared, all those years ago. But her brothers had been taken. It was as if they had died in her place.

"If I could bring back my brothers," she thought, "if I could only bring them back, my father and mother would be happy." She imagined her mother laughing and opening her arms as she welcomed them back. She imagined her father's tears of joy as he hugged each of his sons in turn—and hugged her last and longest.

Just before dawn, the little girl left her bed, and taking only a loaf of bread, a jug of water, and a wooden stool, she went out into the wide world to find her brothers. Over her own blouse she wore her brothers' seven shirts with patterns of the sun, moon, and stars.

"I'll travel as far as the sky is blue," she thought, "and when I meet the sun, he'll tell me if he's seen my brothers."

She marched straight ahead through warm yellow fields, past grazing cows, through berry bushes and brambles, until she came to a murky river with thick grasses growing along its banks. By this time, she was very hot and tempted to take off at least one of the shirts. But she kept on walking.

She followed the river until she came to a cool mossy cave. Placing her wooden stool just inside, she rested. "If I stay here forever," she thought, "it will rain, and the water will rise and I'll disappear, inch by inch."

Suddenly, she felt alone in the world and frightened. Her parents seemed far away. She broke off a bit of bread and, eating it slowly, pictured herself returning home, with her seven brothers by her side. She closed her eyes, trying to imagine what those bird boys looked like, each one older than she and each one bigger and stronger than the next. But the harder she tried, the harder they were to imagine, until, weary with the effort, she fell asleep.

When she woke, the river looked black in the fading light and she sat up, alarmed. She had let too much time slip away. Hurriedly, she took a drink of water from her jug, gathered her things, and edged out of the cave.

"Oh!" she cried, startled, for sitting on a large rock just outside the cave was a round boy, and he was staring at her. His face was rosy, lit from behind by the sunset colors of the sky, and his ears looked too bright, like large pink seashells.

"Sun, oh sun," the little girl cried, "have you seen my brothers?"

The boy yawned and shook his big head.

The little girl came closer. "I must find my seven brothers," she said earnestly, "and bring them home."

"You're a beautiful girl," he said, raising his finger like a torch, "but you shouldn't come too close." Then pointing directly at her, he burned a hole right through her eldest brother's shirt—just over the place on the left sleeve where her mother had sewn the sun.

"If you must know, I am the sun," he said. "Beware, or pretty as you are, I shall turn you to ash."

The little girl screamed and fled, running as fast as she could into the wood, where dark trees cooled the wind that calmed her beating heart.

16

Stumbling on, she heard the sound of distant chimes as twilight deepened into night. In the dimness, she made out the shape of a tall woman coming toward her, carrying in her arms a goat as thin as the crescent moon. A long line of sheep straggled behind, their bells ringing softly.

The little girl knelt until the shepherdess was very close. A cold white light seeped across the forest path. The shepherdess stopped in her tracks, her black robes billowing. The goat fixed its beady eye upon the girl, who shuddered, for suddenly, she felt chilled through and through.

"Moon, oh moon, have you seen my brothers?" she called. The shepherdess shook her head and glided past. The little girl rose up to follow.

"You are brave, little girl, but you shouldn't come too close," the white goat bleated. And it struck the girl a blow with its hoof, ripping a hole in her eldest brother's shirt—just over the place on the right sleeve where her mother had sewn the moon. "If you must know, I am the moon," shrilled the goat. "I am the moon, I am the moon, I am the moon," and its thin voice blended and faded with the sheep bells as the shepherdess bore it away.

18

Sadly, the girl took off her eldest brother's tattered shirt and cradled it in her arms. "I shall never find you now," she whispered dejectedly, tracing her finger along the stitches. The sun her mother had made long ago was burned through and through, and the moon was badly torn, but just below the moon was a straight row of stars, and as she touched them, they seemed to glow slightly.

She gazed up into the black sky. No stars were in sight, but she called out nevertheless: "Stars, oh stars, have you seen my brothers?"

"Yes" came the answer.

The little girl peered into the gloom, and there, not far off, was a dwarf, digging furiously in the earth with a long shovel. On his head was a strange crown, studded with gems.

"Ah, here it is," he cried, holding up a shining sliver of glass as skinny as a needle. "Take it," he said. "It's only a bone, but it may come in handy."

"I've never seen a glass bone before," she said, taking it. And not having a proper place to put the gift, she stuck it into her eldest brother's shirt—just under the spot near the heart, where her mother had sewn the largest star of all.

Then she told the dwarf about her mother and father and her journey in search of her seven brothers and her discouraging meetings with the sun and the moon.

The dwarf listened. "You must love your mother and father very much to have come all this way," he said kindly when she had finished.

The little girl nodded solemnly.

"Your brothers are lucky to have a sister so beautiful, so brave, and so faithful," said the dwarf, touching her shoulder ever so lightly.

"But where are they?" asked the girl. Yet she hardly heard his answer, because all at once, she was spinning up into the air, through the tallest trees, higher and higher into the starry night.

"They live in the Glass Mountain," he called, and his voice sounded far away.

"Oh," called the girl, "and where is that?"

"At the end of the world" came the faint response.

Feeling dizzy, the little girl closed her eyes and let herself turn and turn through black space like a top. When she opened her eyes again, she stood in a long blue banquet hall lined with mirrors. The room was frigid and bare except for seven chairs and a crystal table set for seven.

She shivered and looked for a place to hide, but everything was made of glass except her own jug and stool—and a small dusty baby's rattle hanging on the door.

"Mine!" she whispered, and reached out to touch it.

In her mind, she heard her father's words again: "What's done is done." She had followed her raven brothers to the Glass Mountain. What if she couldn't bring them back?

Trembling, the little girl took off her brothers' shirts and, one by one, placed them on the backs of the chairs. But she kept the burned and torn one, tenderly smoothing it in her hands. Then she crouched down behind her wooden stool to wait.

Before long, she heard thunder rolling toward her and the room turned black. Blindly, she sat huddled in a sudden whirlwind of shadows, as dark as the shadows in her father's eyes.

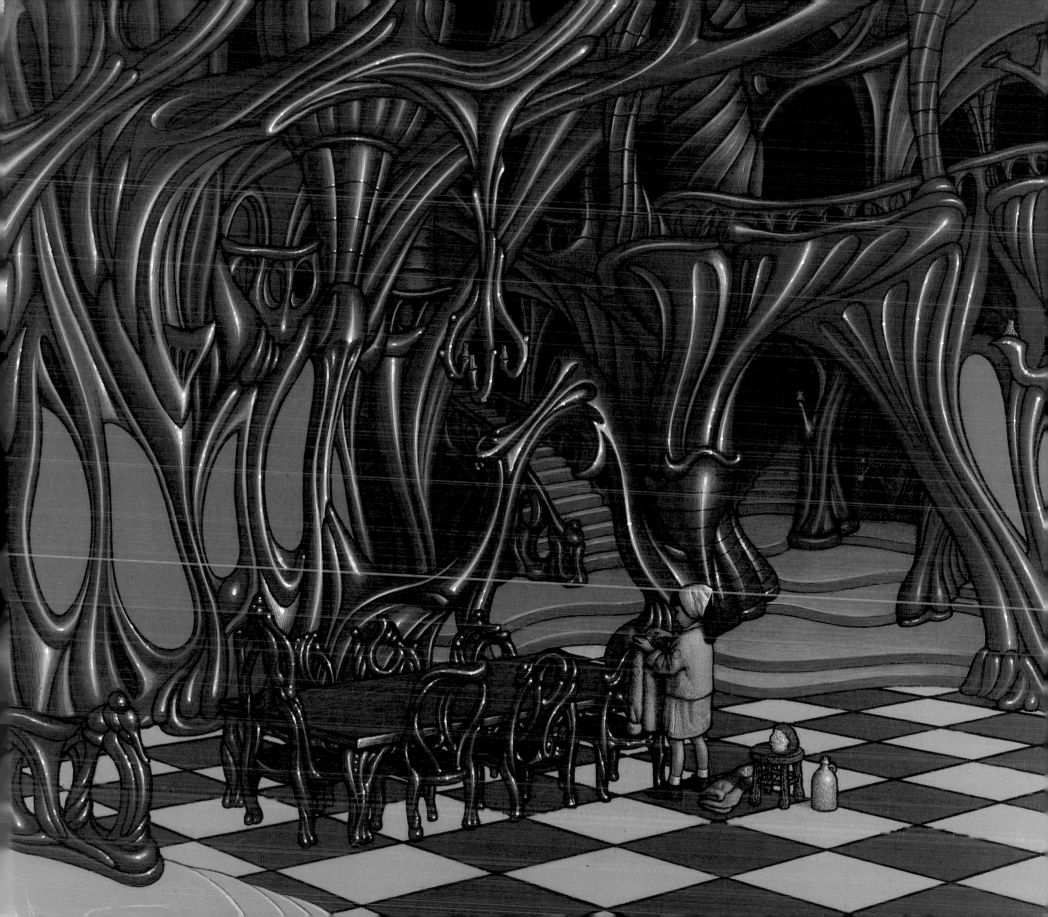

When the thunder subsided, she made out the hulking shapes of six fierce black birds with shining feathers and sharp beaks. They all began to talk at once, until they saw the shirts and fell silent.

"Mother made those," said one.

"To protect us," said another.

"A long time ago," said a third.

"I remember," said the youngest. And he took his shirt in his beak and pulled it over his head.

Lo and behold! His wings turned to arms, his feathers fell off, and he was a boy again! Then all the others did the same, and they too turned back into boys.

Their little sister leaped from her hiding place and ran toward them, giving them each a kiss. But suddenly, she turned pale. "There are only six of you," she said.

No sooner had the words been spoken than the eldest brother limped in, dragging his wings. His left wing was burned; his right wing was broken and torn. And a small wound, like a pin prick, oozed one drop of blood just under his heart.

He stumbled forward but froze when he caught sight of his little sister and all his brothers, who had turned back into boys.

The little girl quickly pulled from under her wooden stool the loaf of bread and the jug of water. "Eat this and drink," she said. And the raven did.

She took the glass bone the dwarf had given her and, unraveling the hem of her own blouse for thread, mended the sleeves of her eldest brother's shirt.

As soon as the little girl had finished, the raven's wings were as powerful as ever. Gently, his sister kissed the wound under his heart.

"Thank you," he said. And just as gently, he placed her on his back.

Then he plucked her baby rattle from its place on the door and shook it triumphantly in his beak.

His brothers climbed on, and they all soared high up above the Glass Mountain into the morning sky. And, like a cloud, the curse of their father's anger lifted. The sun was rising and the moon had not yet disappeared. The little girl held her breath—she had never seen such a sight.

30

On they flew, through clouds and mist, as far as the sky was blue. As evening fell, they landed in a shadowy meadow just outside the village where their parents lived. There, the eldest brother put on his rainbow shirt and turned into a boy.

"We are eight now," he said, smiling. And, together at last, they walked out of the shadows toward home.